A book about Jake

Published in the United States by

Peaks
Press

630 Race Street
Denver, CO 80206
www.peakspress.com

978-1-938032-05-9
Library of Congress Cataloging in Publication LCCN: 2012937206

For Jim, Grace and Blair

My name is **Jake**.

I live on **Drake** Street.

The sun is shining
in the morning
when I **wake.**

I like to eat **pancakes** for breakfast.

It's fun to **rake** leaves in Fall.

In the winter I catch **snowflakes.**

My family takes walks
by the **lake**.

We **make** sandcastles
at the beach
in summer.

I like to shake, shake, shake a tambourine.

When we go to the zoo, I don't like to visit the **snakes**.

If you drop something
it can **break**.

We **bake cupcakes** for
my birthday.

The End

Made in the USA
Columbia, SC
16 December 2020